ATOMIC BOMB PERSPECTIVES

ATOMIC BOMB SURVIVOR STORIES

BY MARTHA LONDON

CONTENT CONSULTANT
Allan M. Winkler
University Distinguished Professor of History (Emeritus)
Miami University of Ohio

Cover image: A mother and child sit in the ruins of Hiroshima, Japan, after the city was bombed in 1945.

Core Library
An Imprint of Abdo Publishing
abdobooks.com

abdobooks.com

Published by Abdo Publishing, a division of ABDO, PO Box 398166, Minneapolis, Minnesota 55439.

Printed in the United States of America, North Mankato, Minnesota
052021
092021

THIS BOOK CONTAINS RECYCLED MATERIALS

Cover Photo: Alfred Eisenstaedt/The LIFE Picture Collection/Getty Images
Interior Photos: Stanley Troutman/AP Images, 4–5, 43; AP Images, 9, 18, 24–25, 34–35, 45; Red Line Editorial, 12, 26; Galerie Bilderwelt/Hulton Archive/Getty Images, 14–15; Keystone-France/Gamma-Keystone/Getty Images, 21; Bettmann/Getty Images, 30; ullstein bild/Getty Images, 36

Editor: Maddie Spalding
Series Designer: Ryan Gale

Library of Congress Control Number: 2019954301

Publisher's Cataloging-in-Publication Data

Names: London, Martha, author
Title: Atomic bomb survivor stories / by Martha London
Description: Minneapolis, Minnesota : Abdo Publishing, 2022 | Series: Atomic bomb perspectives | Includes online resources and index
Identifiers: ISBN 9781532192661 (lib. bdg.) | ISBN 9781098210564 (ebook)
Subjects: LCSH: Atomic bomb victims--Juvenile literature. | Atomic bomb--Juvenile literature. | Nuclear crisis control--Juvenile literature. | Victims of radiation--Juvenile literature.
Classification: DDC 616.9897--dc23

CONTENTS

CHAPTER ONE

A SURPRISE ATTACK

On the morning of August 6, 1945, a US bomber plane headed toward Hiroshima, Japan. The plane was called the *Enola Gay*. It carried an atomic bomb, a type of nuclear weapon.

The day was bright and clear. Air raid sirens had gone off earlier in Hiroshima. The sirens warned of approaching planes. But then the all clear sounded. This sound indicated that the danger had passed.

The atomic bomb destroyed thousands of buildings in Hiroshima, including the Museum of Science and Industry.

So people went about their days. Adults rode the bus to work. Kids played in the schoolyards.

Approximately 43,000 soldiers and 290,000 civilians lived in Hiroshima. There was a military base in the city. At 8:16 a.m., the *Enola Gay* dropped its bomb. Just outside Hiroshima, some people could see the plane. They watched a black dot fall from it. Nothing happened for a few seconds. Then a light flashed. The bomb exploded. People fell to the ground. A strong blast of air flattened trees and buildings. Heat from the explosion started fires and burned people's skin.

EXTREME HEAT

The atomic bombs produced a lot of heat when they exploded over Hiroshima and Nagasaki. The temperature at the center of the explosion reached 1.8 million degrees Fahrenheit (1 million°C). In the area closest to the blast, temperatures ranged from approximately 5,000 to 7,000 degrees Fahrenheit (3,000 to 4,000°C). In comparison, the surface of the sun burns at 10,000 degrees Fahrenheit (5,500°C).

The explosion created a mushroom-shaped cloud. The cloud bloomed high up into the sky. By the time people saw the cloud, the *Enola Gay* was out of sight. Approximately 80,000 people died from the explosion in Hiroshima.

WORLD WAR II

The US military bombed Hiroshima to try to end World War II (1939–1945). The war had been going on for several years. It began in 1939 when the German military invaded Poland. Germany was on the side of Italy and Japan. These countries formed the Axis powers. The Allied powers, or the Allies, opposed them. Great Britain, the Soviet Union, and China were among the Allies.

The United States sent supplies to the Allies. But it did not enter the war right away. On December 7, 1941, Japanese planes bombed a US military base. The base was in Pearl Harbor, Hawaii. Approximately 2,400 US soldiers and civilians died. The United States entered the war the next day. It joined the Allies.

There were two main areas of fighting. The Allies fought Germany and Italy in the European Theater. They fought Japan in the Pacific Theater. The Japanese military had invaded many islands in the Pacific Ocean.

As the war dragged on, US leaders began working on a new type of weapon. In 1942, the US government formed the Manhattan Project. Manhattan Project workers developed the first atomic bomb. An atomic bomb's power comes from atomic chain reactions. This type of reaction happens when atoms split. This process releases a lot of energy. US scientists harnessed and controlled this energy to create the world's most powerful weapon. Officials thought this weapon might be needed to help the Allies win the war.

LITTLE BOY

On May 7, 1945, Germany surrendered. Germany's surrender ended the war in Europe. But fighting

One of the bloodiest battles of World War II happened in Okinawa, Japan. Between 100,000 and 150,000 civilians died. Some civilians surrendered to US troops.

continued in the Pacific Theater. Japan refused to surrender. US leaders were eager for the war to end. They decided that bombing a Japanese city was the best option. They thought this option could help save American lives by ending the war early.

On July 26, the Allies issued a statement. They threatened Japan with destruction if Japanese officials did not surrender. But the statement did not mention the atomic bomb. Japanese officials did not respond to the threat. US leaders prepared to drop the bomb on Japan.

The first atomic bomb was called Little Boy. The center of the bomb was made of uranium. Uranium is a radioactive material. Radioactive materials give off a strong and dangerous type of energy. It remains in soil and water for a long time. Contact with radiation causes sickness. The bomb would have a powerful blast. But it would also release dangerous radiation.

PERSPECTIVES

CAPTAIN ROBERT LEWIS

Captain Robert Lewis was the copilot of the *Enola Gay*. He pushed the button that released Little Boy. The *Enola Gay* crew members believed they were doing their duty. But the power of the bomb surprised them. The explosion flattened Hiroshima. Lewis wrote about the mission in his diary. He said, "If I live a hundred years, I'll never quite get these few minutes out of my mind."

FAT MAN

Three days after the Hiroshima bombing, Japan had still not

surrendered. Manhattan Project workers had created a second atomic bomb. This bomb was called Fat Man. The center of the bomb was made of plutonium. Like uranium, plutonium is radioactive. US officials decided to drop this bomb on Japan.

On the morning of August 9, a US bomber plane flew toward Kokura, Japan. The plane carried Fat Man. The crew initially planned to drop the bomb on this city. But clouds rolled in as the plane flew over Kokura. The pilots could not see the city through the clouds. So they decided to drop the bomb on the secondary target. They flew toward the city of Nagasaki.

Shortly after 11:00 a.m., the crew dropped Fat Man over Nagasaki. Approximately 263,000 people lived in the city. Nagasaki has many hills. The hills protected some parts of the city. However, the bomb still killed many people. Approximately 40,000 people died from the explosion in Nagasaki. Many others died later from injuries and radiation sickness caused by the bombings.

THE ATOMIC BOMBS BY THE NUMBERS

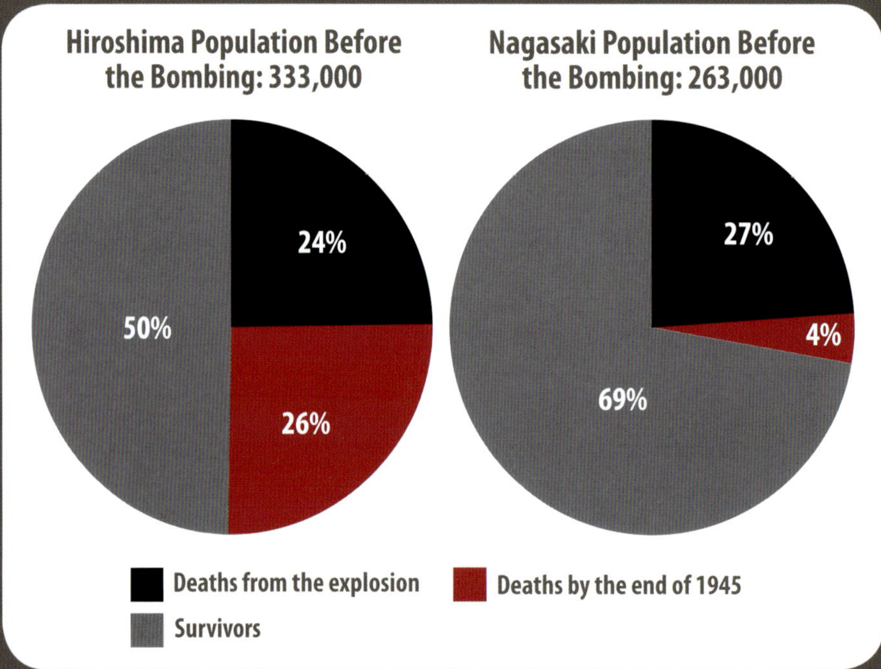

These charts show what percentage of the people in Hiroshima and Nagasaki died from the bombs. Some died from the explosion. Others died later from the effects of the bombings. How do these graphs help you better understand the destruction caused by the atomic bombs?

The bombings did bring an end to World War II. Japanese leaders officially surrendered on September 2, 1945. But the atomic bombs had forever changed the lives of the survivors.

STRAIGHT TO THE SOURCE

Takato Michishita survived the Nagasaki bombing. He was approximately 3 miles (5 km) away from the center of the blast. In an interview, he remembered:

> *An old man yelled 'Plane!' Everyone scurried into their homemade bomb shelters. My mother and I escaped into a nearby shop. As the ground began to rumble, she quickly tore off the tatami flooring, tucked me under it and hovered over me on all fours. . . .*
>
> *When we finally crawled out from under the tatami mat, there was glass everywhere, and tiny bits of dust and debris floating in the air. The once clear blue sky had turned into an inky shade of purple and grey.*

Source: Haruka Sakaguchi. "Mr. Takato Michishita." *1945 Project*, 2019, 1945project.com. Accessed 22 Nov. 2019.

CONSIDER YOUR AUDIENCE

Adapt this passage for a different audience, such as your friends. Write a blog post conveying this same information for the new audience. How does your post differ from the original text and why?

CHAPTER TWO

AFTER THE BLAST

Much of the bombings' effects were immediate. The explosions in Hiroshima and Nagasaki caused extensive damage. Debris spread across the streets. Survivors suffered serious injuries and illnesses. Kiyoshi Tanimoto was one of the survivors. He was a pastor at a church in Hiroshima. He and many others ran in shock through the streets. They searched for their loved ones. Dust covered everything.

A large mushroom-shaped cloud rose over Nagasaki after Fat Man was dropped.

NUCLEAR SHADOWS

The atomic bombs released a bright light when they exploded. When the light hit a solid object such as a person, a shadow was left behind. The shadows formed on walls and floors. People can still see these shadows in Hiroshima and Nagasaki today. The Hiroshima Peace Memorial Museum also preserved some of these shadows. Museum visitors can see the steps of an old bank. On the steps is the shadow of a person using a cane. The shadows remind people of the bombs' intense power.

BURNS

The atomic bomb explosions produced extreme heat. Fires broke out around the cities. Buildings collapsed as they burned. They blocked people's paths. The people who were near the explosions suffered burns. Some of the burns were very severe. Survivors described burn victims walking through the streets. Their arms were outstretched as they tried to keep their skin from painfully rubbing against their clothing. Their skin turned red from the burns.

It was not just the heat that caused burns. Survivors saw a blinding flash of white light as the bombs exploded. This bright light also burned skin. This type of burn was similar to a sunburn.

Many hospitals and other buildings in the cities were destroyed. People looked for help wherever they could find it. Survivors recall burn victims asking for help. They were desperate for water. But many survivors did not understand what was happening. They saw other people who were suffering. But they were afraid and in shock, so they did not stop to help. They wanted to leave the cities and get to safety.

Despite their fear and confusion, some survivors did stop to help others. Kiyoshi saw a woman carrying a child on her back. He led the woman to a school. The school acted as a temporary hospital. Nurses and doctors acted quickly to treat people. But there was a shortage of medical workers. Many had died in the explosions. Others were too injured to work. There had

A survivor and her son lie on the floor of a temporary hospital in Hiroshima in the aftermath of the bombing.

been 1,780 nurses in Hiroshima. Of those, 1,654 had died or were severely injured.

Burn victims were permanently scarred. Many had scars on their face and arms. Some were no longer able to use their hands.

TOXIC WATER

In the aftermath of the Hiroshima bombing, survivors ran to the Ota River. The heat and the dust from the blast caused extreme thirst. Some people drank the river water. Others tried to rinse their burns and cuts. They did not know the river was poisoned. The atomic bomb emitted radiation when it exploded. The radiation made the river toxic. When people rinsed their burns and cuts in the water, they made their injuries worse. Many people got sick from drinking the water.

The river was also filled with debris. The explosion broke apart buildings. Wood, furniture, and other items floated downstream. Bodies also floated past.

BLACK RAIN

Debris and dust particles flew up into the air when the bombs exploded. Radiation and toxic gases also collected in the atmosphere. Only 30 minutes after the bombs exploded in Nagasaki and Hiroshima, rain began to fall. It was not normal rain. The particles in the air had combined with water vapor. The rain contained dust, soot, and radioactive materials. It stained clothes and buildings.

Long after the rain dried, the black stains remained. People could not wash the particles out of their clothing. The survivors' clothes remained radioactive for many years. Toyoko Kubota was 16 years old at the time of the Hiroshima bombing. She kept her black-stained school blouse. In 2018, she donated it to be tested. It still contained small amounts of radioactive material.

PERSPECTIVES

MANHATTAN PROJECT SCIENTISTS

Little Boy and Fat Man were the largest bombs ever made at the time of their dropping. Scientists did not know if they could get the bombs to explode. They did not think about what might happen after the explosion. They did not study the effects of radiation. One scientist explained, "The idea was to explode the [bomb]. . . . We weren't terribly concerned with the radiation."

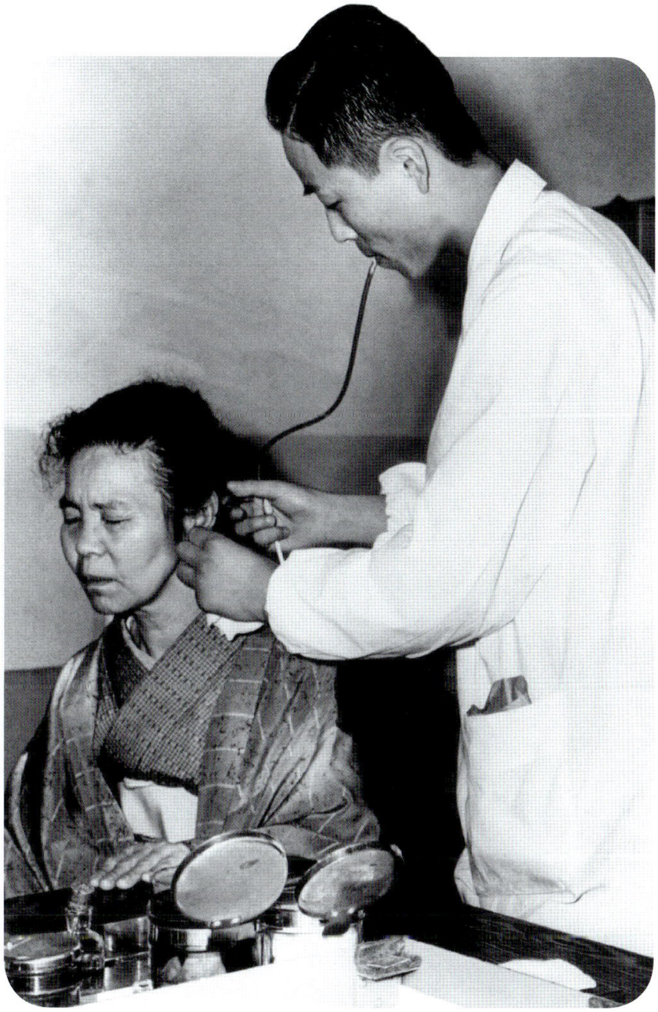

A doctor gives a checkup to a bomb survivor in Hiroshima. Some survivors suffered hearing loss.

RADIATION POISONING

Some people who had survived the bombings became severely ill. People who came to the cities to help also became ill in the days after the explosions. Doctors were not sure what was wrong. They did not understand radioactivity. When scientists built the bomb, they did not completely understand its effects. Radiation poisoning was a new type of sickness. Doctors in Japan did not know how to treat it.

Radiation poisoning attacks a person's cells. As a result, the person's body is unable to work normally. People who had radiation poisoning lost their hair. Some began to bleed from their gums. Their injuries did not heal.

Radiation exposure often causes cancer. Many people who survived the bombings later developed cancer. Doctors found a high rate of leukemia among survivors. Leukemia is a type of blood-related cancer. Lung cancer and many other types of cancer were also common among survivors. Cancer treatments were limited in the 1950s and 1960s, causing many people to die from the disease. Researchers estimate that 140,000 people died from causes related to the bombings by the end of 1945.

STRAIGHT TO THE SOURCE

Shizuko Mitamura was in Nagasaki the day the atomic bomb was dropped. She was three years old at the time. In an interview, she explained how the bombing affected her and her loved ones:

> *I myself was diagnosed with colon cancer when I was 39. . . . I overcame the disease, only to be diagnosed with cervical cancer when I was 59.*
>
> *My second oldest sister was diagnosed with colon cancer, twice. My third oldest sister was diagnosed with rectal cancer and passed away at age 39. Their daughters have also passed away in their 30–40s due to cancer and a brain tumor. These are all members of my household who were exposed to the atomic bomb.*

Source: Haruka Sakaguchi. "Ms. Shizuko Mitamura." *1945 Project*, 2019, 1945project.com. Accessed 22 Nov. 2019.

BACK IT UP

The author of this passage is using evidence to support a point. Write a paragraph describing the point the author is making. Then write down two or three pieces of evidence the author uses to make the point.

CHAPTER THREE

LONG-TERM EFFECTS

Japanese people called the atomic bomb survivors *hibakusha*. This means "atomic-bomb-affected people." The hibakusha faced discrimination after the explosions. Many people thought radiation poisoning was contagious. They thought it could spread through air or by contact with another person. For this reason, they avoided interacting with the hibakusha. Survivors also had trouble finding jobs. Many employers would not hire them.

Children in Hiroshima wore masks to protect themselves from air pollution caused by the bombing.

CANCER AMONG HIROSHIMA SURVIVORS

This graph shows the number of Hiroshima survivors who developed cancer between 1958 and 1998. Many of these cases can be linked to radiation exposure from the bomb. Which types of cancer were most common? How do you think cancer and other sicknesses affected the survivors?

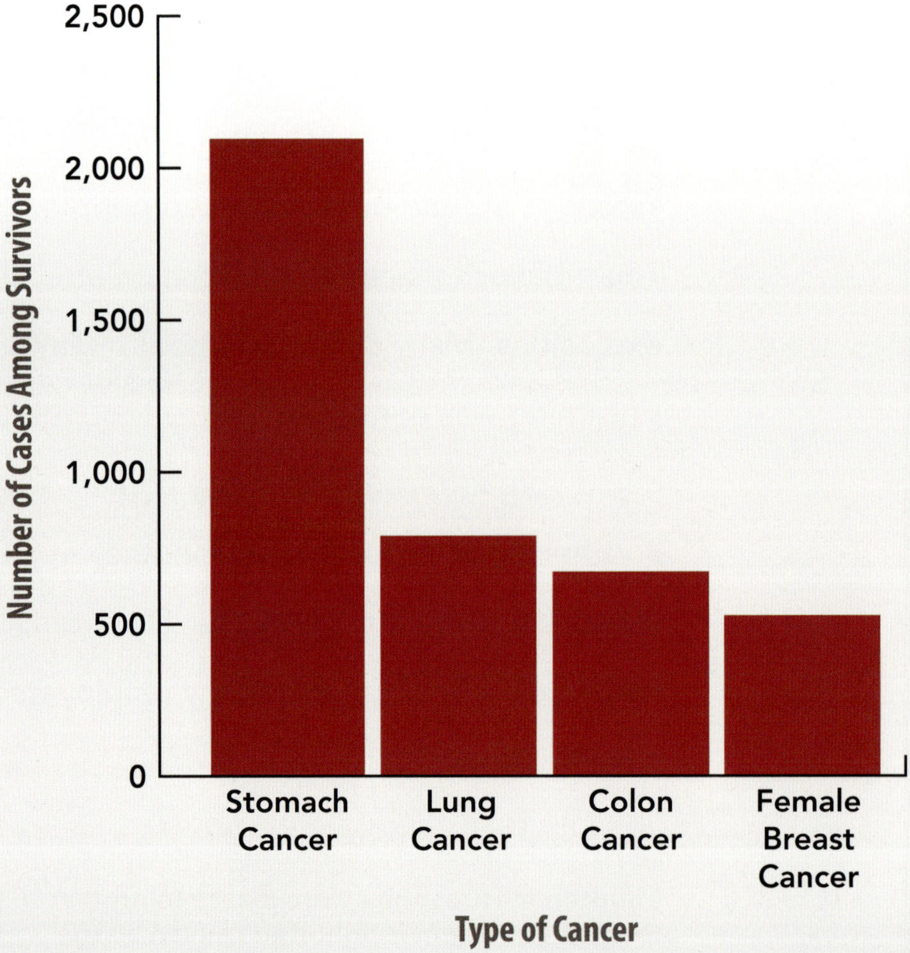

In addition, medical knowledge about how to treat radiation was limited. No one knew what the long-term effects of the bombings were. Many health care workers also thought radiation poisoning could spread, so they refused to treat survivors. The hibakusha often did not have access to medical care.

Survivors also had lasting mental health issues. They suffered a great deal of loss. Many people lost their loved ones. They also lost their homes and businesses. This affected their mental health. Many people felt guilty for surviving. They did not understand how they could be alive when so many others had died.

Some hibakusha were children when the bombs exploded. Their parents died in the attack. They grew up as orphans. Many survivors suffered from depression. Depression is an intense feeling of sadness and hopelessness. This feeling lasts a long time.

Many survivors moved away from Nagasaki and Hiroshima. These cities no longer felt like home.

They tried to start new lives elsewhere in Japan. Many lied about their past. They wanted to avoid discrimination. Some even kept their past a secret from their spouses and children.

People feared radiation poisoning could be passed down to children. Doctors and scientists were not sure what would happen if bomb survivors had children. They also thought the hibakusha could infect their spouses. For these reasons, many people believed the survivors should not be allowed to marry

PERSPECTIVES

HELPING SURVIVORS

Tomin Harada was a Japanese doctor. He grew up in Hiroshima. He was in Taiwan when the United States bombed Hiroshima. But he returned to the city after the war. He performed surgeries to help survivors who had scars. The surgeries helped fix some of the scars. He also advocated for the survivors. He asked the Japanese government to cover survivors' medical expenses.

Harada's wife was in Hiroshima during the bombing. She later died from cancer. Harada believed radiation had caused the cancer.

or have children. Even some hibakusha shared these beliefs. They were afraid of passing illnesses or birth defects on to their children. They did not want their children to face discrimination like they did.

DENIAL

At first, US officials thought the Japanese people were lying about radiation poisoning. They claimed the bombs exploded far enough from the ground that radiation would not affect the survivors. News from Japan was also slow to spread out of the country. The United States occupied Japan after the war. US officials created censorship laws. These laws restricted what Japanese reporters could say about the bombs. They also prevented news sources from publishing photos of the cities after the bombings. Also, many survivors did not share their experiences because they feared discrimination. For these reasons, it took awhile for many people to learn about the bombs' effects. Over time, other countries learned more about the bombings.

Survivors who had visible scars often faced discrimination.

Then Americans realized that Japanese doctors were not lying.

In 1947, US president Harry S. Truman formed the Atomic Bomb Casualty Commission (ABCC). This was a group of scientists and doctors. It was clear the world needed more information about the effects of the atomic bombs. The ABCC studied atomic bomb survivors. Doctors from the United States and Japan worked together on this study. The study was important. It helped doctors and scientists learn how radiation affected people. However, the study caused some controversy. Doctors ran blood tests on thousands of hibakusha. But American doctors were not allowed to treat survivors because US officials thought this would seem like an apology for the bombings. Many people thought this

THE HIROSHIMA MAIDENS

In 1955, 25 Japanese women traveled to the United States. They had survived the Hiroshima bombing. Some people called the group the Hiroshima Maidens.

The women came to the United States to undergo plastic surgery. Plastic surgery involves reconstructing features, such as lips, using skin from other parts of the body. Plastic surgery technology was better in the United States than it was in Japan. Over the course of 18 months, doctors performed 140 surgeries on the women. Most of the surgeries were successful. The women regained the use of their fingers. Doctors made their scars less noticeable.

was wrong. They believed doctors had a duty to treat their patients. Some American doctors did treat the hibakusha. But many did not.

TELLING THEIR STORIES

It took time before survivors could talk about their experiences in Hiroshima and Nagasaki. Reporters helped them share their stories with the world. John Hersey interviewed six survivors. These interviews were published in a *New Yorker* article in 1946. The article gave people a firsthand look at the bombs' effects.

The censorship laws ended in 1952. Soon afterward, *Life* magazine published photos of the mushroom cloud from the Hiroshima bombing. The magazine also published a story about the hibakusha and their experiences. It was one of the first times people outside of Japan saw the effects of the atomic bombs.

The *Life* story helped change how people viewed the survivors. Before, many people had treated them as outcasts. But after the story was published, people around the world wanted to know about the hibakusha. The hibakusha began to tell their stories. They wanted people to understand the damage the atomic bombs had caused.

EXPLORE ONLINE

Chapter Three discusses the discrimination the hibakusha faced. The website below shares some of their stories. As you know, every source is different. What information does the website give about the survivors? How is the information from the website the same as the information in Chapter Three? What new information did you learn?

CHILDREN OF THE ATOMIC BOMB

abdocorelibrary.com/survivor-stories

MARCH
LONDON
ALDERMASTON
FROM ALDERMASTON
TO UNITED NATIONS
VIA
平
和
PATIENTS OF "A"
SEND THEIR
THE HIROSHIMA
PEACE

CHAPTER
FOUR

HOPE FOR PEACE

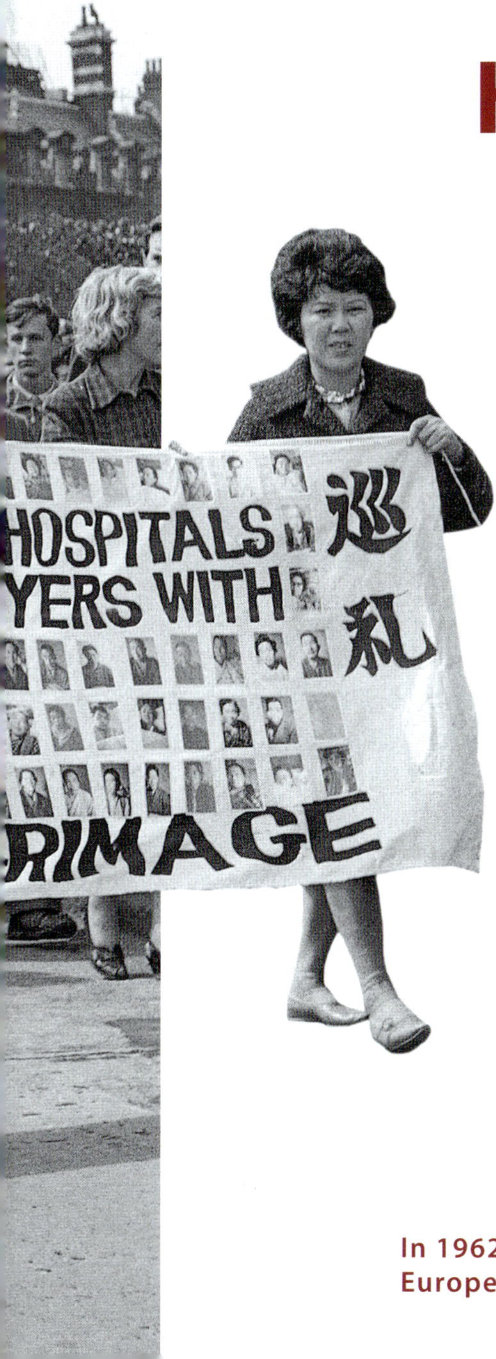

In 1962, some atomic bomb survivors marched in Europe to protest nuclear weapons development.

Today, the atomic bomb survivors are getting older. The bombings happened more than 75 years ago. But they continue to tell their stories. The bombings affected their lives in many ways. Some of these effects can still be seen in Hiroshima and Nagasaki.

ENVIRONMENTAL IMPACTS

The bombings damaged the environment in Hiroshima and Nagasaki.

It took approximately four years to clear debris and rebuild Hiroshima after the bombing.

The force of the explosions caused widespread damage. The blasts were strong enough to rip trees from the ground. Radiation poisoned the water and soil. Plants absorbed the radiation from the soil. People could not grow crops. The explosions also killed or affected many animals, including those that people relied on for food. Fish absorbed the radiation from the water. They were too toxic to eat.

Despite these challenges, the people of Nagasaki and Hiroshima rebuilt their cities. Today, there is little remaining radiation in these areas. It is safe to live in the cities. But while the land has largely recovered, many survivors continue to suffer health problems such as cancer.

PERSPECTIVES

SURVIVOR AND ACTIVIST

Sunao Tsuboi was 20 years old when the bomb hit Hiroshima. Today, he educates people about nuclear weapons. He does not want other people to experience what he went through. Tsuboi worries another nuclear attack could happen. In a 2015 interview, he said, "People like me are losing the strength to talk about their experiences and continue the campaign against nuclear weapons."

NIHON HIDANKYO

Some survivors are part of a group called the Nihon Hidankyo. This organization was created in 1956 during the Second World Conference against A- and H-Bombs. The conference was held in Nagasaki. Thousands of survivors and activists attended. They advocated for the end of nuclear weapons testing. The conference has continued every year since then.

There have been no other nuclear attacks since the Hiroshima and Nagasaki bombings. But some countries have large supplies of nuclear weapons. The United States has more than 5,000 nuclear weapons. Experts estimate that Russia has nearly 6,000 nuclear weapons. Other countries around the world also have nuclear weapons. Countries keep supplies of nuclear weapons to protect themselves in the event of an attack. However, the Nihon Hidankyo and many Japanese people believe no country needs nuclear weapons. There are other ways to protect countries and keep people safe. For this reason, the Nihon Hidankyo continues its work. Activists travel around the world. They educate people about the bombings and promote peace.

Japan's leaders created a new constitution after World War II ended. US officials helped write this document. Article 9 of the constitution states that Japan will not get involved in any more wars. Today, Japanese officials work to solve conflicts peacefully. Japan does not have a large military. It also does not have nuclear weapons.

WITHIN THE CITIES

The legacy of the bombings is still visible in Hiroshima and Nagasaki. The cities have memorials dedicated to the people who died in the bombings. In Hiroshima, a large museum has exhibits about the bombings. Visitors can learn more about what Hiroshima was like before and after the bombing. In Nagasaki, a park was created to promote world peace. It is called

A THOUSAND PAPER CRANES

Sadako Sasaki survived the Hiroshima bombing. She was only two years old at the time. She was later diagnosed with leukemia. In Japanese culture, cranes represent good health. One legend said if a person folded 1,000 paper cranes, he or she would be granted a wish. So Sadako tried to fold 1,000 paper cranes. She wished for peace. She died at the age of 12, before she could finish the task. Her classmates folded the remaining cranes. Sadako's parents buried her with the cranes. There is a memorial dedicated to Sadako at the Hiroshima Peace Memorial Park. People place paper cranes on her memorial.

the Nagasaki Peace Park. The Nagasaki Atomic Bomb Museum shares the story of the bombing on August 9.

More than 1.5 million people visit the Nagasaki and Hiroshima memorials each year. Japanese people also remember the bombings in other ways. Each year on the anniversary of the Nagasaki bombing, the city's mayor reads a peace declaration. The mayor discusses any steps that have been taken to try to eliminate nuclear weapons.

Today, some survivors and their children try to get payment for their medical expenses. They ask US and Japanese organizations to help cover these expenses. They argue that they should not have to pay for their cancer treatments. It is likely that radiation exposure from the bombings caused the cancer. Organizations such as the Nihon Hidankyo have been successful in getting some of the survivors' medical expenses covered.

Survivors and activists want to prevent another nuclear attack. They want to show the world that people today still suffer from the effects of the atomic bombs. These effects echo on into later generations. Many survivors know they will not live to see the end of nuclear weapons. But through their strength and persistence, survivors have helped educate people about the effects nuclear weapons have on humanity.

FURTHER EVIDENCE

Chapter Four describes the lingering effects of the atomic bombs. What was one of the main points of this chapter? What evidence is included to support this point? Read the article at the website below. Does the information on the website support the point you identified? Does it present new evidence?

SURVIVORS OF HIROSHIMA AND NAGASAKI

abdocorelibrary.com/survivor-stories

IMPORTANT DATES

December 7, 1941
Japanese planes bomb a US military base at Pearl Harbor, Hawaii. The next day, the United States enters the war on the side of the Allies.

July 26, 1945
The Allies issue a warning statement. They threaten to attack Japan if Japanese officials do not surrender.

August 6, 1945
The *Enola Gay* plane drops the Little Boy atomic bomb on Hiroshima, Japan. Approximately 80,000 people die from the explosion.

August 9, 1945
The US military drops the Fat Man atomic bomb on Nagasaki, Japan. Approximately 40,000 people die from the explosion.

September 2, 1945
Japanese leaders officially surrender, ending World War II.

1947

US president Harry S. Truman forms the Atomic Bomb Casualty Commission (ABCC). The ABCC studies atomic bomb survivors.

1956

Thousands of survivors and activists attend the Second World Conference against A- and H-Bombs in Nagasaki.

STOP AND THINK

Tell the Tale

Chapter One of this book explores what happened on the day of the Hiroshima bombing. Imagine you are visiting Hiroshima a few days after the explosion. Write 200 words about the destruction you see and people you meet. What could you do to help?

Surprise Me

Chapter Three discusses the survivors' experiences and the long-term effects of the bombings. After reading this book, what two or three facts about these effects did you find most surprising? Write a few sentences about each fact. Why did you find each fact surprising?

Say What?

Studying war and nuclear weapons can mean learning a lot of new vocabulary. Find five words in this book you've never heard before. Use a dictionary to find out what they mean. Then write the meanings in your own words and use each word in a new sentence.

Take a Stand

Today, many survivors and their children have radiation-related illnesses. They continue to try to get coverage for their medical expenses. Do you think governments or organizations should pay for these expenses? Why or why not?

GLOSSARY

advocated
supported a cause

censorship
describing something that suppresses or silences information that is thought to be harmful

civilian
someone who is not a member of a country's military

discrimination
the unjust treatment of a group of people based on their race, gender, or other characteristics

nuclear
relating to an atom's nucleus, or the central part of an atom

radiation
a harmful energy produced by materials such as uranium

tatami mat
a floor covering made of a strawlike material

toxic
describing something that is poisonous

ONLINE RESOURCES

To learn more about the atomic bomb survivors, visit our free resource websites below.

Core Library CONNECTION
FREE! COMMON CORE MULTIMEDIA RESOURCES

Visit **abdocorelibrary.com** or scan this QR code for free Common Core resources for teachers and students, including vetted activities, multimedia, and booklinks, for deeper subject comprehension.

Booklinks NONFICTION NETWORK
FREE! ONLINE NONFICTION RESOURCES

Visit **abdobooklinks.com** or scan this QR code for free additional online weblinks for further learning. These links are routinely monitored and updated to provide the most current information available.

LEARN MORE

Huddleston, Emma. *How the Bomb Changed Everything*. Abdo Publishing, 2022.

Murray, Laura K. *World War II Technology*. Abdo Publishing, 2018.

INDEX

About the Author

Martha London writes books for young readers full-time. When she isn't writing, you can find her hiking in the woods.